Freddie and Flossie and the Easter Egg Hunt

Visit us at www.abdopub.com

Spotlight, a division of ABDO Publishing Company, is a school and library distributor of high qualit
reinforced library bound editions.

Library bound edition © 2006

Library of Congress Cataloging-in-Publication Data

Hope, Laura Lee.
Freddie and Flossie and the Easter egg hunt / by Laura Lee Hope; illustrated by Maggie Downer.—1st e
p. cm.—(Bobbsey twins) (Ready-to-Read)
Summary: Twins Freddie and Flossie have a hard time finding Easter eggs when their dog Snap is
around.
ISBN-13: 978-1-4169-1029-9
ISBN-10: 1-4169-1029-8
[1. Twins—Fiction. 2. Brothers and sisters—Fiction. 3. Easter eggs—Fiction. 4. Easter—Fiction.
5. Dogs—Fiction.] I. Downer, Maggie, ill. II. Title. III. Series.
PZ7.H772Fpu 2006
1-59961-100-7 (reinforced library bound edition)

All Spotlight books are reinforced library binding and manufactured in the United States of Americ

The BOBBSEY TWINS®

Freddie and Flossie and the Easter Egg Hunt

by Laura Lee Hope

illustrated by Maggie Downer

Ready-to-Read

Aladdin

New York   London   Toronto   Sydney

Easter is here!

Freddie and Flossie

are on an Easter egg hunt.

Flossie looks under a flower.

No egg here.

Freddie looks beside a rock.

No egg here.

Flossie looks under a shrub.

No egg here.

Freddie looks in a tree.

Oops!

Where are the eggs?

See Snap.

Snap has the eggs!

Silly Snap!

Easter egg hunts
are for kids, not dogs!